Put Beginning Readers on the Right Track with
ALL ABOARD READING™

The All Aboard Reading series is especially for beginning readers. Written by noted authors and illustrated in full color, these are books that children really and truly *want* to read—books to excite their imagination, tickle their funny bone, expand their interests, and support their feelings. With four different reading levels, All Aboard Reading lets you choose which books are most appropriate for your children and their growing abilities.

Picture Readers—for Ages 3 to 6

Picture Readers have super-simple texts, with many nouns appearing as rebus pictures. At the end of each book are 24 flash cards—on one side is the rebus picture; on the other side is the written-out word.

Level 1—for Preschool through First-Grade Children

Level 1 books have very few lines per page, very large type, easy words, lots of repetition, and pictures with visual "cues" to help children figure out the words on the page.

Level 2—for First-Grade to Third-Grade Children

Level 2 books are printed in slightly smaller type than Level 1 books. The stories are more complex, but there is still lots of repetition in the text, and many pictures. The sentences are quite simple and are broken up into short lines to make reading easier.

Level 3—for Second-Grade through Third-Grade Children

Level 3 books have considerably longer texts, harder words, and more complicated sentences.

All Aboard for happy reading!

For Garrett—J.D.

To my parents, Peggy and Joe Church B.E.M.
—P. C.

Library of Congress Cataloging-in-Publication Data

Dussling, Jennifer
    Gargoyles : monsters in stone / by Jennifer Dussling ; illustrated by Peter Church.
        p. cm. — (All aboard reading. Level 2)
    Summary: Describes different kinds of gargoyles, how they are created, and how they
function as waterspouts.
    1. Gargoyles—Juvenile literature. [1. Gargoyles.] I. Church, Peter, ill. II. Title.
III. Series.
    NA3683.G37D87 1999   98-42133
    729' .5—dc21   CIP
                                                                              AC

ISBN (pb) 0-448-41961-0 A B C D E F G H I J
ISBN (GB) 0-448-41962-9 A B C D E F G H I J

ALL
ABOARD
READING™

Level 2
Grades 1-3

Gargoyles

MONSTERS IN STONE

By Jennifer Dussling
Illustrated by Peter Church

Grosset & Dunlap • New York

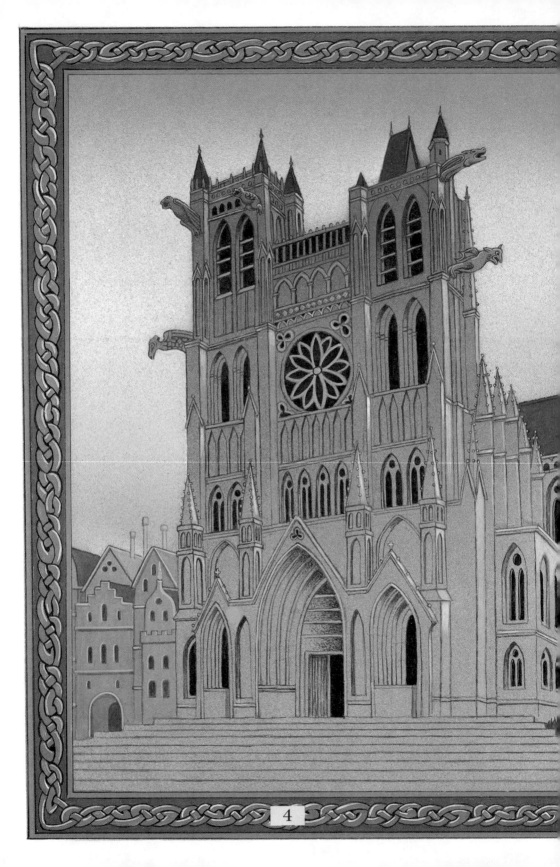

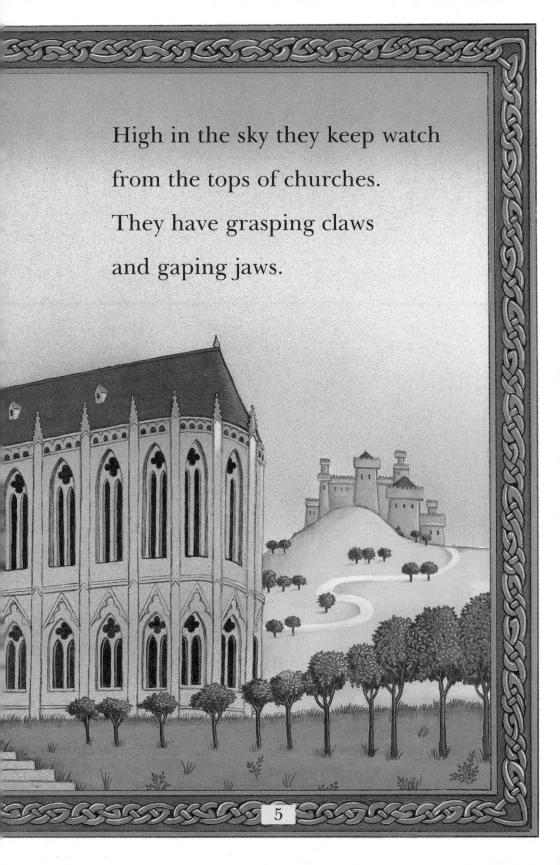

High in the sky they keep watch

from the tops of churches.

They have grasping claws

and gaping jaws.

Look closely and you will see
that monsters lurk.

They are monsters of stone—
gargoyles.

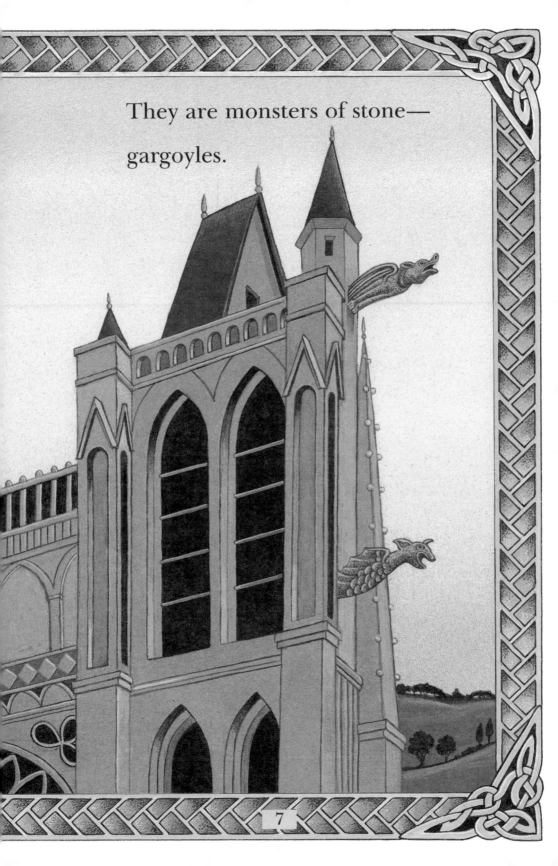

A gargoyle

(you say it like this: GAR-goil)

is a stone statue

that is weird or strange-looking.

They were very popular

in the Middle Ages,

back in the time of knights and castles.

Many gargoyles are found on churches.

In the Middle Ages,

the church was the most important place

in every town.

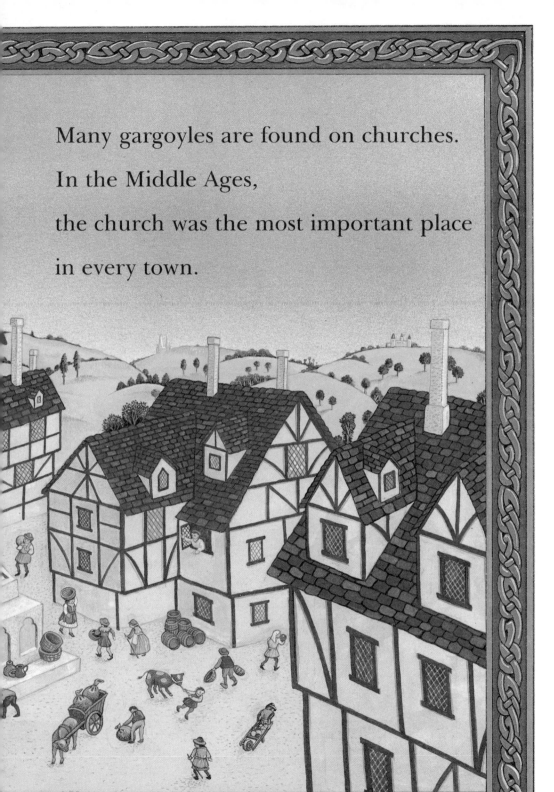

People were proud of their churches.

So builders filled every corner,

inside and out, with stone statues.

Inside the churches were statues
of Jesus, Mary, and the saints.

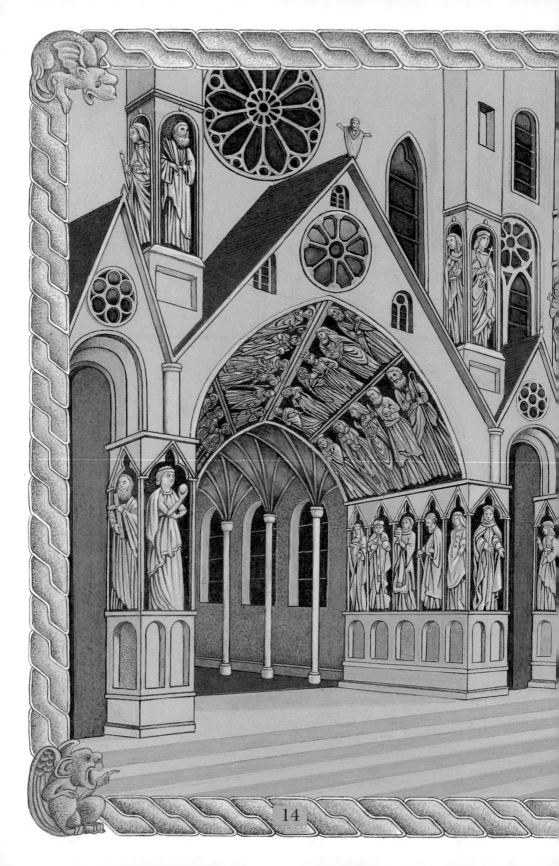

Outside there were statues
of holy people, too.

But high up above the holy people,
near the very tops of the churches
were the gargoyles.

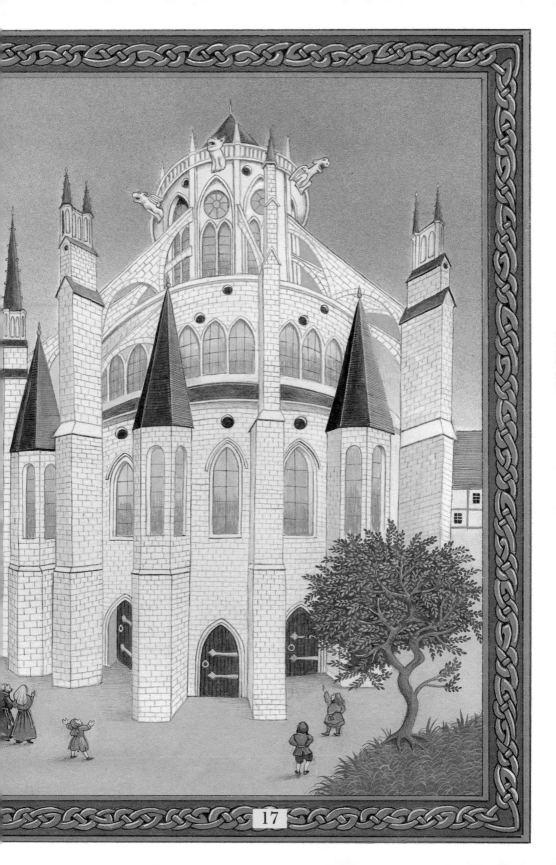

Why would anyone carve a monster

on a church?

Some people think it was

to scare people into being good.

Other people think gargoyles

kept away evil spirits.

The fact is we don't know exactly why
they look like they do.
But we do know
what gargoyles were used for.
They drained off water.
Rain could wear away
the stone of a church.
So gargoyles kept the water
away from the church's walls.

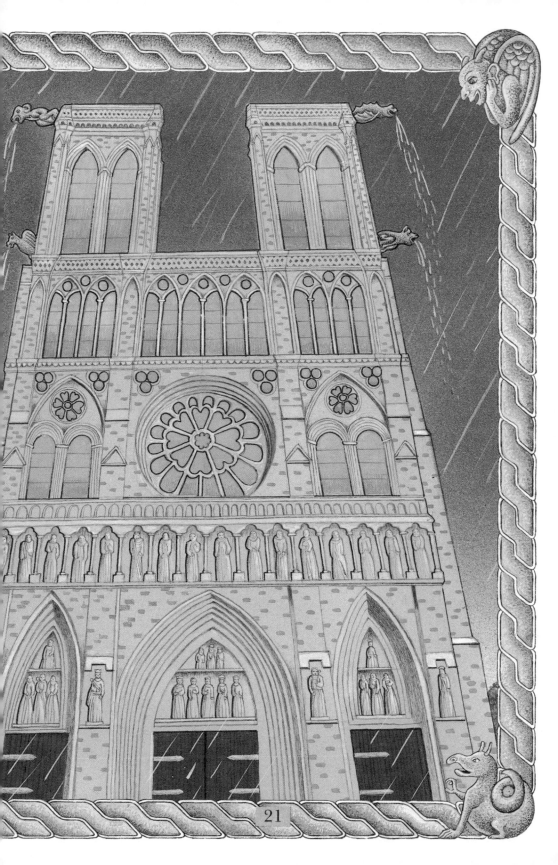

They were like fancy, funny drainpipes.

Rain ran through the pipes

in their bodies.

Then it shot out their mouths!

That is how gargoyles got their name.

"Gargoyle" comes from a French word

that means "throat."

And think about it.

Gargoyle sounds a lot like

the word "gargle."

And that is what gargoyles did.

They held water in their mouths.

Then they spit it out.

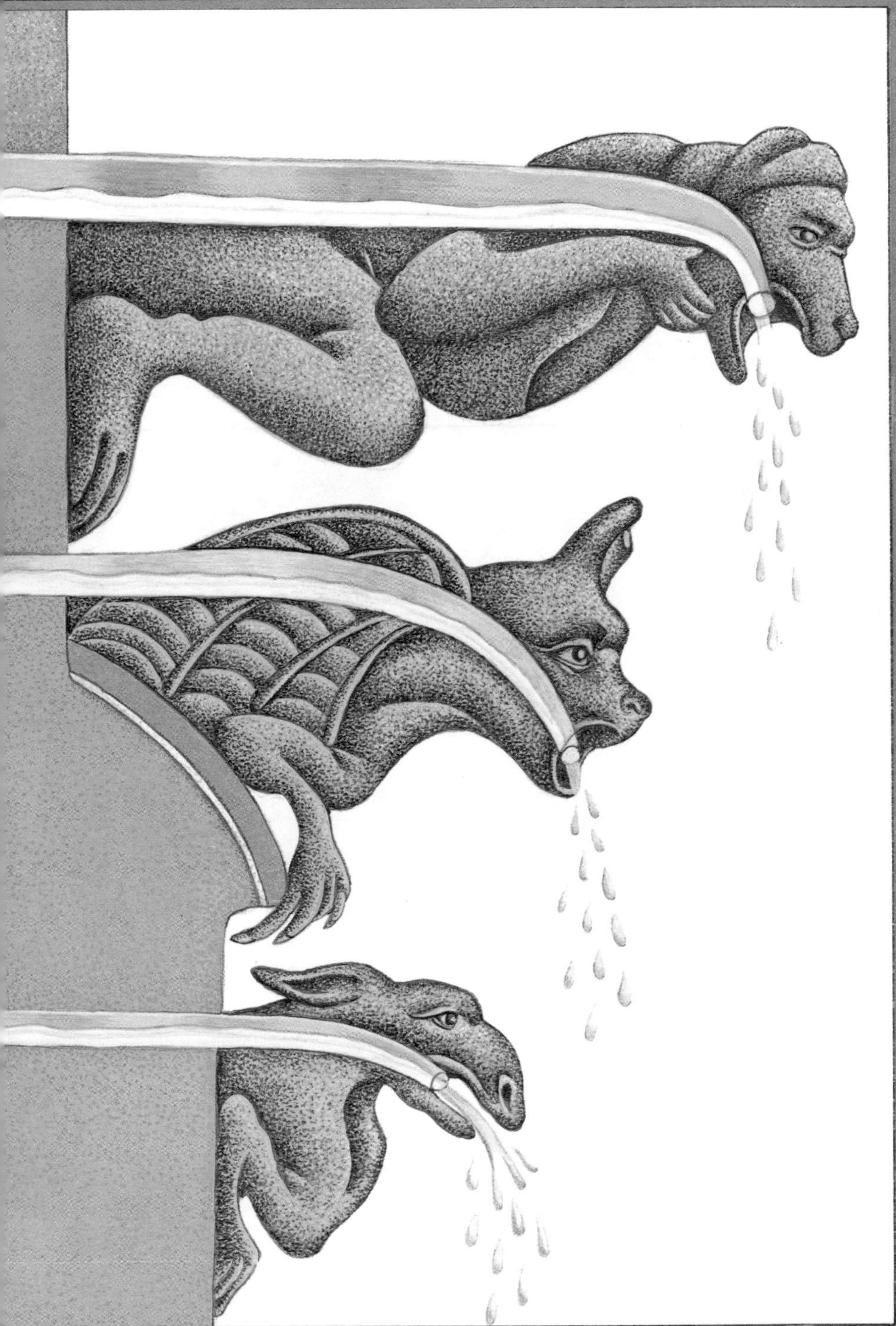

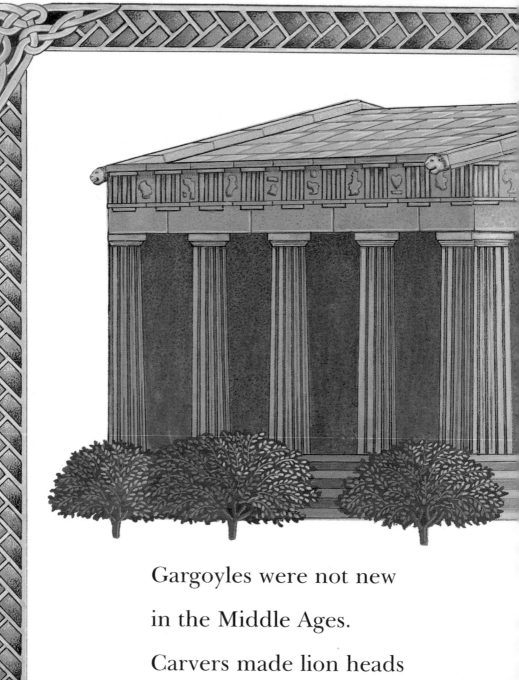

Gargoyles were not new

in the Middle Ages.

Carvers made lion heads

on Greek temples.

There were also

animal waterspouts

in ancient Egypt.

Most people think of a gargoyle

as a monster.

But gargoyles can be people.

Some are

happy

people...

silly people...

scary people.

This gargoyle is
pulling his mouth open
and sticking out his tongue!

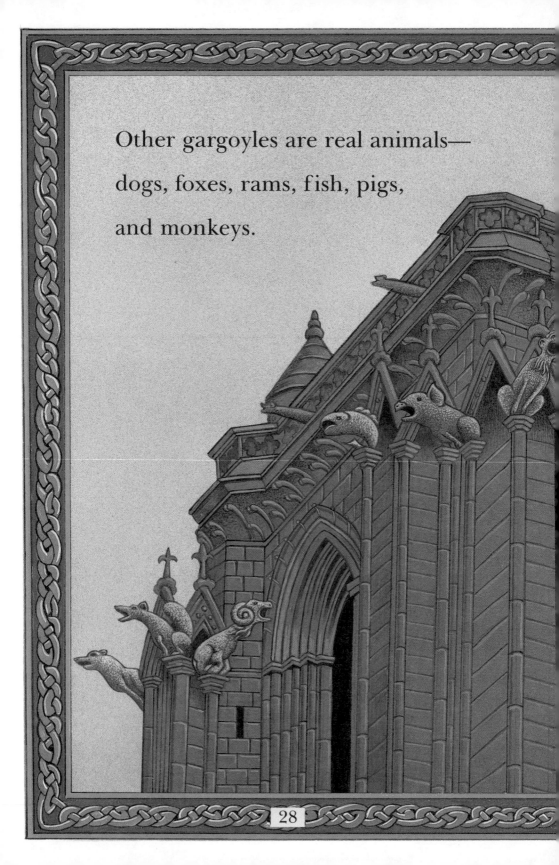

Other gargoyles are real animals—
dogs, foxes, rams, fish, pigs,
and monkeys.

Some were a mix of animals.

Or half person and half animal.

Here is a lion gargoyle.

It doesn't look much like a lion.

The man who carved it

probably never saw a real lion.

He may have heard of lions.

Maybe he pictured one in his head.

Or maybe he saw a drawing

in a book.

It was hard work to carve a gargoyle.

First the carver picked

a block of stone.

Then he took some

chalk and drew

the gargoyle on it.

Because gargoyles are so high up,

they can be hard to see.

So carvers made

big, wide mouths.

They made deep eyes.

They gave the gargoyles

extra-long noses and ears.

That way even far down below,
people still could see the faces.

What tools did stone carvers have?

Just hammers, chisels, and drills.

Rock is very hard.

A carver had to sharpen

his tools all the time.

The carver worked on the ground.

He did not carve high up on the church.

That would be too dangerous.

A piece of rock could fall

and hurt somebody.

When the gargoyle was all done,
workers would put it in place.

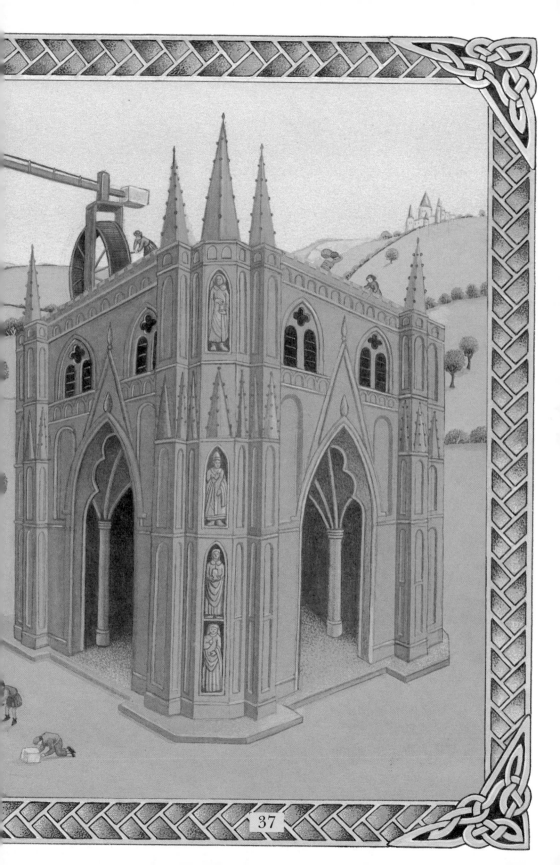

Carving was hard work.

But it was probably fun, too.

For the statues of saints and holy people,

the carvers had to follow rules.

But for a gargoyle,

a carver could do what he wanted.

Sometimes it was a way

to poke fun at a person.

We think some old gargoyles

are based on real people.

Who does this gargoyle look like?

The most famous gargoyles
in the world are in Paris.
They perch high up
on a huge church.
It is called Notre Dame
(you say it like this: No-tra Dahm).

There are elephants

and panthers and goats.

There are monsters, too,

with horns and wings and hooves.

Many are very scary.

They watch the people below.

They look like they will fly down

at any moment.

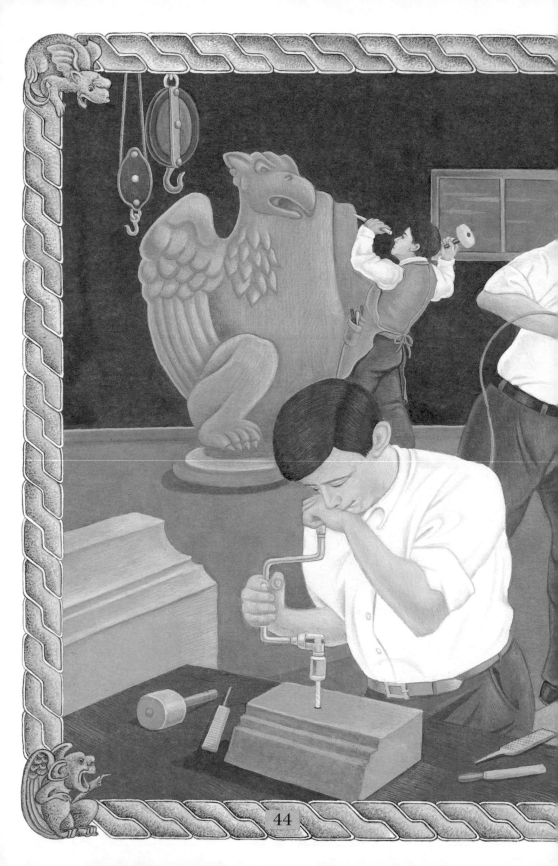

Gargoyles still are carved today.

And carvers still use the same tools—

chisels, hammers, and drills.

But they have modern tools, too!

This church is in Washington, D.C.

It was started in 1907.

And it still isn't done!

It will have lots of gargoyles.

People can even get

their very own gargoyle.

A dentist gave a lot of money

to the church,

so a special gargoyle

was made for him.

It is a man cleaning a BIG tooth!

You don't have to go far

to see a gargoyle.

There could be some in your town.

So don't forget to look up.

A gargoyle may be watching <u>you</u>!